Richard Scarry's
THE SNOWSTORM SURPRISE

A GOLDEN BOOK • NEW YORK

Western Publishing Company, Inc., Racine, Wisconsin 53404

Huckle Cat and
Lowly Worm look out of
the window.

It is raining outside.
Leafless winter tree
branches blow in the
winter wind.

Mother Cat has asked the boys to
tidy their room. It is not much fun.

"Why doesn't it ever snow?" Huckle asks Lowly. "All it does is rain."

"If it snowed," Lowly says, "what fun we could have outdoors! We could go sledding and skiing.

"We could build a snow
fort and make a snowman!"

Just then Mother Cat comes into the room.
"My, what a neat room!" she says.
"You boys must not have had
time to look out the window."

Outside it has begun to snow! Big white snowflakes tumble down. They stick to the ground and turn everything white.

"Can we play outside,
Mother?" Huckle asks.
"I want to ski!" says Lowly.

"You will need a lot of snow for that," Mother
replies. "You may have to be patient. In the meantime,
you can taste the snowflakes." She bundles the boys
up warmly and sends them out to play. Then she
begins to make a cake in the kitchen.

It is snowing very hard.

"Shall we make a snowman?"
Huckle suggests.
The boys busily roll balls of
snow around the yard.

Lowly asks Mother Cat for a carrot for the snowman's nose, cookies for the eyes and buttons, and a bright red scarf for the snowman's neck.

By the time they have finished, the snow is already deep. Huckle and Lowly are cold and wet. They decide to warm themselves inside the house.

Mother Cat hangs their wet clothes near
the stove and makes them hot cocoa.
There is a knock at the door.

It is the Three Beggars: Harry Hyena, Benny Baboon, and Wolfgang Wolf. "Mother Cat," says Harry Hyena, "we are very cold and hungry. If we shovel your drive, would you have something for us to eat?"

Mother Cat invites them inside and serves
them cocoa and cookies.
"Thank you, Mother Cat," they say.
Mother Cat puts the cake in the oven.

A yellow light flashes
outside. It is the snowplow.

It makes a loud noise—
CRUNCH! Then it comes
to a halt.

Again there is a knock at Mother Cat's door.
It is Mr. Fix-It.

"Hello, Mother Cat," he says. "It is snowing
so hard, I can't see where to plow. May I rest for
a moment, please?"
Mother Cat invites Mr. Fix-It in.

"How good it smells in here!"
says Mr. Fix-It. "What are
you baking?"

"A cake," Mother Cat replies.
"Snowstorm Cake."

As Mother Cat pulls the cake out of the oven,
there is another knock at the door.

"Who can it be this time?" she wonders.
It is Mr. Frumble. "Oh, do please excuse me,"
he says. "I wonder if I could telephone Mr. Fix-It.
Someone has parked a snowplow on top of my car."

Mother Cat invites
Mr. Frumble inside.

Huckle and Lowly want to go outside again. The snow is now so deep, the snowman is buried up to his neck!

The boys try to pull the sled. Then they try to walk on skis. But it is no use. They sink deep into the snow.

"Now I think we have TOO MUCH snow!"
Huckle says with a laugh.

They go back inside and make drawings of
the snowstorm to show Father Cat when he gets
home from work.

There is yet another
knock at Mother Cat's door.
It is Sergeant Murphy.

"Hello, Mother Cat," he says. "I wonder if you can help. The Busytown bus is stuck in the snow. The passengers are cold. Could they warm up here until the storm has passed?"

Mother Cat invites the bus passengers inside.

Finally the kitchen door opens without a knock.
It is Father Cat, home from work.
"Happy birthday, Father Cat!"
everyone sings.

What a surprise!

The house has been decorated, and candles burn atop the Snowstorm Cake. Everyone has a wonderful time. They all agree that Snowstorm Cake is delicious.

And . . . it is Father Cat's biggest birthday party ever!